Stay With Me While I Go To Sleep

– TAMSYN CHAMBERS –

Tamsyn Chambers

FASTPRINT PUBLISHING
PETERBOROUGH, ENGLAND

STAY WITH ME WHILE I GO TO SLEEP
Copyright © Tamsyn Chambers 2010

ISBN 978-184426-794-1

First published 2010 by
FASTPRINT PUBLISHING
Peterborough, England.

Printed in England by
www.printondemand-worldwide.com

PREFACE

I know you and have felt you grow as I grow.
It is not long now.
I am part of you but not yet free to be me.
My pulsing heart grows stronger as I feel you making her for me.
You know I am your baby girl but they all said I'd be a boy.
I cannot wait to hold her.
You know how I need to hold her soft rag body close to me.
I yearn to move my fingers over her hair, hair like yours that flows over me and outside of me.
She tells me her hair is green.
I do not know what green is, but feel you lavish it, smooth it and talk to it, as if it were me.
She has become your baby, but soon it will be me.
Then how happy I shall be.

CONTENTS

The Noisy Tomato Plants

Once upon a time there was a pretty little girl called Miranda. She was a very good little girl and every evening before she went to bed would help her Mummy to water the plants in the study.

The study was a room just like any other room but in the middle of it was a huge table covered in pots. In each pot was a small seedling. The seedlings were tomato plants which one day would grow very big and produce lots of tomatoes to eat for dinner.

Sometimes Mummy would give Miranda a small watering can so that she could water the plants all on her own.

One evening, Miranda went into the study on her own to water the plants. They had been getting taller and were now about an inch tall with some leaves forming. Suddenly, the silence was broken by a noise. "I'm bigger than you," said a whisper. Miranda looked everywhere but could not see anyone. Then she heard a little voice say, "Rubbish I'm bigger than you". Again Miranda looked round but could not see anyone and assumed that her imagination was playing tricks on her, because she was tired.

The next evening Miranda went to water the plants again. They had all grown and produced several more leaves. "Hello Miranda" said a voice. Miranda was so startled that she nearly dropped the watering can. Perhaps, just perhaps, the plants were talking to her. Then another deeper voice said, "I'm bigger than all the rest – look at me". Miranda looked at all the plants carefully and then she could see quite clearly that the plants were moving as they talked. One plant was plainly much bigger than the rest and waved its leaves shouting "Hello Miranda, I'm glad you've seen me now – but that's because I'm bigger than the rest".

The next evening, Miranda knew what to expect. "Hello plants" she said when she entered the room. "Hello" replied a lot of small voices. The plants continued to argue about whom the biggest were and were so noisy that Miranda wondered if her Mummy could hear them. She thought it would be nice if Mummy did know about the talking plants.

The next evening, Miranda took Mummy to see the plants. They entered the room but everything was quiet. Miranda thought the plants must be shy and did not bother to take Mummy in again.

It was not long before miniature tomatoes began to form on some of the plants. "My tomatoes are bigger than yours," said a voice. The small tomatoes began to swing angrily and got redder.

Very soon all the plants had big juicy red tomatoes on. Mummy was very pleased and praised Miranda for looking after the plants so well.

The next day Mummy gave everyone tomato soup for tea and put a large bowl of luscious red tomatoes in the larder.

That evening Miranda opened the study door. A sudden silence hit her. The room was empty apart from one tomato plant that had failed to grow any tomatoes. Miranda's eyes filled with tears but then a little voice said "Don't cry – we'll see you again next year – we did well, didn't we, enjoy the tomatoes". At that the little plant seemed to crumple up and land in a dry brown heap of dust in its pot. But Miranda was no longer sad – the plants had done their job and would return next summer. Perhaps they would talk to Mummy next year.

The Birthday Cocktail

It was the first time that Miranda had been on holiday on her birthday. She was with her Mummy and Daddy and her six year old sister on a Greek island called Zakynthos. Tomorrow she would be nine years old.

The day of her birthday came. That evening Miranda and her family went into the hotel restaurant for dinner. At dinner Miranda was amazed when the head waiter suddenly appeared holding an enormous birthday cake with nine lit candles on it. The cake had white icing with chocolate sponge and cream inside. There were sugar swans and mountains on it and it had "Happy Birthday Miranda" written in jam.

Miranda had no difficulty in extinguishing all the candles in one giant blow, after which everyone started to eat large mouthfuls of cake.

After a little while, Miranda bit into something hard. She stopped eating and felt into the cake with her fingers and pulled out a small tin bottle labelled "Birthday Cocktail."

Miranda treasured the bottle all through the holiday, keeping it safely in her pocket. She took it back on her aeroplane to England.

On the aeroplane, Miranda suddenly heard some Greek music, but she did not know where it was coming from. An air hostess went up to Miranda and told her off for having a radio on in the aircraft. Miranda was mystified but then realised that the music was coming from her small tin bottle that she had found in her cake. When she examined the bottle, she discovered that there was an on-off switch on the outside of the bottle which had somehow got into the on position. Miranda quickly turned the switch to the off position and then forgot all about it.

When Miranda had been at home for a few days, she suddenly remembered the bottle. She called her sister Francesca and got out the bottle from her pocket. Miranda turned the switch to the on position and lovely Greek music started playing. Francesca started to nag Miranda to open the screw top lid on the top of the bottle. Miranda was hesitant, so Francesca threatened to pinch and bite her if she did not open it immediately and be sharp about it. After a chase around the house and some abrupt words from Mummy, Miranda opened the bottle.

Black smoke rushed out of the bottle and filled the room. Mummy came in and was very cross. "What are you doing?" she screamed. "We are only playing" said Francesca. Satisfied, Mummy returned to the computer room. Then Miranda and Francesca heard lots of voices coming from the bottle. The mist cleared and they saw fairies sitting round a large table covered in party food.

There were sausages, crisps, sandwiches and cakes and small cups of juice. Two of the chairs at the table were bigger than the rest and were vacant. One had a label saying

Miranda and the other had a label saying Francesca. The two children sat on the chairs and joined in the feast.

Greek music started and all the fairies began dancing on the table.

Suddenly a fierce voice shouted "Get off the table and be sharp about it." The voice came from a cross looking elf. All the fairies except one got off the table. The elf was so cross that he magicked all the chairs, the table and the naughty fairy who was still dancing on the table, back into the bottle.

All the fairies started to dance on the floor. Miranda asked where her presents were. Each of the fairies gave Miranda a small parcel and then vanished.

Miranda said to Francesca "Shall I open my presents?" "Go on" said Francesca. "Open them and be sharp." So Miranda opened all of them and in each parcel, she found a small tin bottle labelled "Birthday Cocktail". Each bottle had a number on from ten to thirty.

The Pedalo

The family was on holiday at Zakynthos, the Greek island where turtles breed.

One day, they decided to have a go on a pedalo, a small boat with two sets of pedals.

Miranda and Francesca wore sunhats as the sun was hot and sat at the rear, while their parents pedalled in front.

Soon the pedalo was right out to sea and the girls looked down through the clear blue water in search of turtles.

Suddenly, Miranda's sunhat fell off right into the sea. Her Daddy leaned over and tried to grab it as it floated by the pedalo. Unfortunately, he had been eating a lot of moussaka and as he leant over so did the pedalo which tipped right over onto its side, throwing the four occupants into the sea.

Fortunately everyone had lifejackets on, but very soon the pedalo had sunk out of sight.

For a while, the four swam about in the sea and were just about to despair when they saw a miniature island not too far from them.

The island was just a few rocks joined together. The four swam towards the island and clambered onto it.

To their amazement, they discovered they were sharing this miniature island with a small turtle. Then all of a sudden, they realised that the island was moving. It was floating in the sea and as they looked out over the vast sea, they noticed a multitude of other small islands of varying sizes also floating in the sea around them.

Some of the islands had several fully grown turtles on them and the islands all seemed to be going in the same general direction.

There was nothing else to do but sit tight as there was no sign of any other land.

After about an hour, a stretch of coastline could be seen. However, as they got closer, it became apparent that it was made up of lots of small islands which had joined together. All the islands seemed to be heading towards this stretch of land until they too joined up with it.

Once the island had stopped moving, the four walked across the rocks onto the main land and saw hundreds of turtles lazing there in the warm sunshine.

The land had lots of trees and seemed fertile with wild berries and fruit trees with apricots growing in abundance.

"We will have to build a raft" said Daddy. So they set about finding branches that had fallen from trees and used weeds to weave the wood together.

After a couple of hours and several apricots later, the raft was finished. Daddy found some branches to be used as oars.

They all pushed the raft across the sand to the water's edge and got on.

Soon they were rowing out to sea. Daddy looked at the direction of the sun and his watch to steer the raft. After about two hours, Zakynthos was in sight. They were safe.

To their surprise, the lost pedalo was sitting safely anchored on the shore. The man hiring the pedalos seemed to be excited and said something about a six foot turtle pushing it to shore. Mummy said it could not possibly be true.

The next day the family went to a talk on the conservation of the turtles and discovered that there are a few years in a turtle's life when they completely disappear and no one knows where they go. "We will keep their secret safe" Miranda whispered to Francesca.

The Twelfth Night of Christmas

It was the same night that Daddy had taken the Christmas tree into the garden, in fact the twelfth night of Christmas that the strange happenings occurred.

Miranda was in bed with Cornelius, her toy bunny rabbit. It had been such an exciting Christmas with all those presents and the Christmas tree covered in lights and decorations. She had felt quite sad when Daddy took down the Christmas tree and all the tree decorations and took the tree into the garden. Daddy said it was unlucky to keep the tree in the house any longer.

As Miranda looked at Cornelius, she could suddenly hear strange noises coming from the garden, though she could not quite make out what they were. All she could tell was that they sounded bubbly and excited. "Cornelius" said Miranda, "Go and investigate." Cornelius was a good bunny rabbit. He hopped down from Miranda's bed and went quietly into the garden.

Cornelius could not believe his eyes. In the middle of the garden was the Christmas tree ablaze with fairy lights and it was very definitely walking up the garden. When Cornelius became accustomed to the darkness and looked

more carefully, he saw that twelve bunny rabbits were carrying the tree. They carried it to the top of the garden by the holly bush. Cornelius followed the tree.

By the holly bush there was a whole circle of garden animals - all the bunny rabbits of whom he could recognise Johnny Bunny and Fat Bunny. There was also the whole Nutty family of squirrels, several unknown birds, a hedgehog and numerous toy teddy bears. They were all chattering ten to the dozen and sounded very excited but they did not notice Cornelius.

Suddenly, everybody started to dance round the Christmas tree and sing and then the animals played Musical Chairs and other exciting games such as Musical Pine Needle, Hunt the Pine Needle and Pass the Pine Needle.

Mummy Teddy Bear was in evidence too. She was very busy cooking. She had two very large pots, each with a large wooden spoon. One pot had Pine Needle soup and the other Pine Needle Pie. Every now and again she would cut a small branch off the Christmas tree and put it in one of the pots. "More Pine Needle Pie?" she said to Mummy Nutty Squirrel. Mummy Nutty Squirrel jumped about a foot into the air, and her fur went into goose pimples as she screeched "Not more Pine Needle Pie!"

Suddenly everything went silent. The clock could be heard shrieking "Boing, Boing, Boing ----------" There were twelve boings. It was twelve midnight.

Immediately, the Christmas tree lights went out and everybody scurried off home.

Cornelius thought he had better go home and tell Miranda all about it. He crept back quietly into Miranda's bed, but she was fast asleep. She never did find out about those strange happenings after all.

Cornelius is Naughty

It was summer and Mummy liked to have lunch in the garden on hot sunny days. Daddy was stuck in the office all day and wanted some fresh air at lunch time and baby Miranda enjoyed crawling in the garden at any time.

On one such sunny day, Mummy had prepared a delicious lunch of salad. She set out three dishes on the large garden table. At the bottom of each dish she placed several large lettuce leaves. Next were radishes, tomatoes and cucumber, some grated carrot and lots of eggs and cheese.

Daddy came home for lunch and took Mummy and Miranda into the house to bring out some chairs.

While everybody was in the house, Cornelius bunny rabbit just happened to hop into the garden. Well, when he saw the table with three dishes containing lettuce and radishes, he just could not resist it. He jumped onto the table and went up to the first dish. He started to nibble the lettuce, then the radishes and before long he had eaten all the salad, just leaving the eggs and cheese.

He had never tasted anything quite so delicious. Then Cornelius went to the next dish and finally the third dish

and once more ate all the salad. After eating all that lunch, Cornelius was so full that he collapsed exhausted in the middle of the table and fell right off to sleep.

Mummy, Daddy and Miranda had at last found some suitable chairs and brought them into the garden. They were all hungry and looking forward to some lunch. However, when they reached the table, they were horrified to see that their dishes were empty apart from the eggs and cheese. Baby Miranda began to scream and cry out "Oh no where's my lunch?" and Daddy looked aghast and screeched "Who has stolen our lunch?" Then Mummy suddenly saw that naughty bunny rabbit Cornelius asleep on the table. He was snoring loudly and he had remains of lettuce and tomato pips all over his whiskers.

Version for children:

Mummy poked Cornelius "Wake up, wake up" she snapped angrily. But Cornelius would not wake up. He just grunted a little and continued to snore.

Mummy poked him again and shouted even louder. "Wake up you naughty bunny rabbit, you have eaten all our lunch." Eventually one eye opened and then shut again, then the other eye opened and shut again. Then both eyes opened followed by a collapse of two ears which succeeded in hiding the two open eyes. "What is the meaning of this?" said Daddy. Cornelius began to speak slowly, still half asleep and very dazed. "What is wrong?" he said slowly. "Is something wrong?" "You are a naughty rabbit" said Mummy. "What are you going to do to make up for eating our lunch?"

Cornelius began to realise he had in fact behaved very badly and began to feel guilty. "Well I have a very large sack of carrots at home" he said. "You could have some of those." "That will do nicely" said Mummy. "Get them at once."

Cornelius went off to get the carrots. When he returned Mummy rushed off with the carrots and was soon busy in the kitchen. A few minutes later, Mummy returned with carrot soup in a large bowl.

Everybody, even Cornelius enjoyed the carrot soup. Mummy was a good cook. Nobody asked how she had turned carrots into soup so quickly.

After lunch, Mummy, Daddy, Miranda and Cornelius had forgotten the earlier events and danced round the garden singing songs. They were all friends again.

Version for fed up parents:

Mummy picked up the sleeping Cornelius and carried him into the house.

A few minutes later she returned to the garden with a big bowl.

"Lunch at last" she said to Daddy and Miranda.

The lunch was delicious, but Cornelius was nowhere to be seen!!!!

Caterpillar Soup

Once upon a time, Miranda was playing in the garden. She had been very busy pulling up weeds for her Mummy and was beginning to feel a little bit hungry.

It just so happened that at that very moment Hoppity Bunny Rabbit came along. "Hello Miranda" said Hoppity Bunny Rabbit "Would you like to come to a party by the greenhouse? All the animals are there." Miranda hoped there might be some food at the party and accepted the invitation.

When Hoppity and Miranda reached the greenhouse, a whole host of people were there. There were lots of bunny rabbits, teddy bears and several rag dolls. Mummy Teddy bear was busy cooking something very hot in a large pot and was stirring it with a large wooden spoon.

Then everybody including Miranda sat down round Mummy Teddy and waited to be fed.

Mummy Teddy dished up what looked like delicious smelling soup into numerous dishes and handed the dishes complete with spoons round to everyone. Miranda was delighted when she was handed a dish. "It looks good" said Hoppity who was sitting next to Miranda.

Miranda put her spoon into her dish and filled it with soup. She was just about to put the spoon into her mouth when, to her horror, she noticed something moving in the soup. "What is this?" she cried out. When she looked closer, she could see numerous legs and green fur! It was a caterpillar. Before she could say another word, Hoppity snatched up the caterpillar and ate it. "Lovely" said Hoppity "Don't you like caterpillars?" Miranda was too polite to say anything but just filled her spoon again and put it to her mouth. She felt something hard. When she looked at the spoon, there was a .... snail in it. Before she was able to gasp in horror, a rather fat thrush swooped down nearly knocking her off her balance, took the snail into his beak and flew off in haste.

Miranda politely filled her spoon again wondering what she would find next – she was so hungry. This time something slimy slithered across the spoon. "Oh no it's a slug" thought Miranda. But before Miranda shrieked, the slug slid off the spoon back into the dish of soup. Miranda filled her spoon again. She was beginning to be a little fed up with this soup. This time something long wriggled up the handle of the spoon. It was a long wriggly worm. Suddenly a large blackbird swooped down and picked up the worm in its beak and flew off.

By now Miranda had had enough. She stood up, thanked Mummy Teddy for the party and excused herself, saying it was time she went into the house.

When she went into her house, she was very pleased to see her Mummy cooking lunch in the kitchen. "What's for lunch mum?" she asked.

"Soup" said her Mummy. Miranda's face fell and tears streamed down her face. "Whatever is wrong?" asked her

Mummy. "There aren't any caterpillars in it are there?" she cried.

"Of course not" said her Mummy.

Needless to say Miranda enjoyed her cabbage soup and I am pleased to say there were no caterpillars, snails, slugs or worms in it. At least if there were, they were all cooked!

Penny's Haircut

Once upon a time there was a rag dolly called Penny. She had beautiful long green hair.

One day however, Penny was very unhappy because her hair had grown so long that it reached her ankles and she kept falling over it. Her legs were covered in bumps and bruises from tripping over.

Penny sat down in the garden and began to weep so that huge tears watered the daisies on the lawn. Well just at that very moment who should come along but Hoppity Bunny Rabbit. Hoppity was called Hoppity because for some strange reason one of his four legs was shorter than the others so that he ran with a jerky hop.

"Hello" said Hoppity to Penny. "Whatever is the matter? Why are you crying?" Penny explained how her hair was so long that she kept falling over it and hurting herself. "Poor Penny" said Hoppity. "Why don't you go to the hairdresser and get your hair cut?" Penny explained that she had no money and you needed money to pay for a haircut.

Suddenly Hoppity had a wonderful idea. "Penny" said Hoppity "You know that I have very sharp teeth – well I

have to in order to eat carrots – well I could nibble your hair until it is short enough for you."

Penny was delighted and agreed to the wonderful idea.

Hoppity stood by Penny's feet and started to nibble her hair. He nibbled and nibbled and nibbled. Lunch time came and went, teatime came and went and eventually he had nibbled Penny's hair so that it only reached her waist.

Penny was overjoyed with her haircut. She thanked Hoppity giving him a great big kiss.

Well after that, whenever Penny's hair grew too long, she went to see Hoppity for a haircut. Hoppity did not mind at all because it helped to sharpen his teeth and anyway he did not like to see Penny unhappy. Very soon Penny had the tidiest hair ever seen.

The Naughty Caterpillars

Once upon a time, there was a grey bunny rabbit called Cornelius. He lived in a hole in a tree trunk in a very large garden.

Every day Cornelius would visit the cabbage patch for his lunch. He was very fond of cabbages. He usually ate one cabbage for lunch and then had tea with Hazel Squirrel who lived at the top of a large nut tree in the garden.

One day Cornelius went to the cabbage patch for his lunch. When he got there, however, he saw that there was a plague of caterpillars all over the cabbages. All the leaves were full of holes. He knew the owners of the garden would be very cross indeed and he himself was not very pleased. He did not like cabbages with holes in nor did the cabbages taste nice after caterpillars had been chewing them.

Cornelius sat by the patch looking very sad. Just at that very moment who should come along but Hazel Squirrel. "What's the matter?" asked Hazel.

Cornelius explained about the naughty caterpillars. "Isn't there a hose in the garden?" asked Hazel. "Yes" replied Cornelius.

Hazel and Cornelius dragged the hose up to the cabbage patch and Cornelius turned on the tap. Between them, they managed to hose down the cabbages. All the caterpillars floated off the cabbages and were swept away in a stream of water which settled in a big puddle behind the greenhouse.

Cornelius was so pleased. The cabbages tasted nice and juicy from the fresh water. In fact they had never tasted so good.

Hazel was pleased because Cornelius was pleased and they both celebrated by dancing around the lawn and singing the Cabbage song.

"Won't you sing along
Cos this is the cabbage song.
If you eat your cabbage all up
It's all you need for supp
----------- "

The Woodpecker

Daddy Squirrel lived with his family in a large nut tree in the garden. Every day he would climb down the tree and collect nuts for supper.

One day, Daddy Squirrel was just about to climb down his tree when he heard a very strange noise – "Peck, peck, peck – peck, peck, peck." Whatever could it be? Daddy looked down the tree and near the bottom was a very naughty woodpecker. The woodpecker had been pecking at his tree and had already made a small hole in the bottom of the tree trunk.

Daddy Squirrel stayed at the top of the tree and began to cry. His tears dripped down the tree trunk and fell onto the woodpecker's head. However, the woodpecker thought it was raining and continued to peck at the tree.

Well just at that very moment, who should come along but Cornelius Bunny Rabbit. He could see Daddy Squirrel's tears falling onto the woodpecker's head. "Whatever is the matter?" shouted up Cornelius. Daddy Squirrel explained that the woodpecker had already made a hole in his tree and if the woodpecker carried on pecking, he might peck right through the tree until it fell down. If that happened, Daddy Squirrel would have nowhere to live. Also, he was frightened to climb down his tree in case the woodpecker took a peck out of him.

Cornelius sat down near the tree and started to think. You could almost see the wheels in his brain turning because his eyes kept revolving as he thought. After thinking for some time, Cornelius suddenly knew what he must do. He got up and went to the bottom of Daddy Squirrel's tree. Very quietly he crept up behind the woodpecker's tail and then he started to nibble the end of the tail. Now as you may know, Bunny Rabbits have very sharp teeth. That is because they eat chewy things like raw carrots and raw cabbage and do not eat sweet things which spoil their teeth.

Well when the woodpecker felt someone nibbling his tail, he did not like it one bit. He flew away with a sudden gust. He flew and flew as fast as he could and he did not stop until he was a very long way away. What is more he never returned to Daddy Squirrel's tree.

You can imagine how pleased Daddy Squirrel was. He climbed down his tree and thanked Cornelius by giving him a large nut. As Cornelius was a Bunny Rabbit, he did not like nuts at all, but took it out of politeness and gave it to a passing magpie.

As for Daddy Squirrel, he was so tired that it was all he could do to gather a few more nuts and climb up his tree to bed. It did not take him long to get to sleep.

Miranda's Monster

Once upon a time there was a little girl called Miranda. One day she walked to school along the same town pavements. It was a day just like any other day, but she just happened to notice a hole in one of the pavement slabs. She thought some workmen must have left it there but still peeped down at it in case it held hidden treasure. To Miranda's utter astonishment, two green tentacles appeared, quickly followed by a yellow prickly face. A "monster!" she thought in horror.

The monster stared at Miranda, who by now found she was glued to the spot through fear. "Don't be afraid" said the monster in a rather feeble voice for such an awe inspiring sight. "My name is Fred. May I come to school with you? I've always wanted to go to school." By this time, Miranda's fear had vanished. That fierce-looking monster was a softy and she felt rather sorry for him. "Yes, you may come" replied Miranda and Fred the monster followed behind Miranda all the way to school.

When Miranda got to school, she left the monster in the playground while she went into her classroom. She asked the teacher, Mrs Nott, if she could bring her monster to school. "Don't be silly" said Mrs Nott "there are no such things as monsters." "But," said Miranda "it's outside in the playground." To keep the peace, Mrs Nott, in a most disbelieving voice told Miranda she could bring the monster in. "Oh by the way" said Miranda "he's called Fred."

Miranda went to the playground and told the monster it could come into the classroom. Fred entered the classroom greeted by thirty speechless children and Mrs Nott looked somewhere between being about to explode and faint. "Well" shrieked Mrs Nott "I don't believe it. He'll have to be good and sit at a desk and work as hard as everyone else."

So that morning Fred sat at his own desk next to Miranda and burying his green tentacles in his workbook, appeared to be working away with his sums.

At the end of the morning, Mrs Nott went round to look at all the children's work. "Miranda" she said "I am afraid that six plus six are twelve and not seven." Next Mrs Nott came to Fred's desk. To her disgust, she found that Fred had been drawing, and not doing sums. Instead of writing the number twelve, he had drawn twelve little baby monsters, all replicas of himself and beautifully coloured in. However, before Mrs Nott had a chance to gasp, Fred stood up holding his masterpiece in the air and twelve baby monsters stepped off the page and started chasing each other in-between and on top of the desks, singing tunes at top voice.

"Silence" and "be still" screeched Mrs Nott. "All monsters are expelled from the school at once." Without another noise or dance, Fred and his babies went up to

Miranda, with tears in their slimy eyes and as it was lunchtime, Miranda thought she had better take them all home.

They all obediently and silently followed Miranda as she went back along those same town pavements, but when Miranda looked behind her, one by one each baby monster popped down into a separate hole in the pavement. Finally Fred gave Miranda a cheery wave as he too disappeared into a somewhat larger hole.

Miranda was a little sad to have lost her new friends and wondered how all the holes had vanished. She went back to check they really had gone and then went on alone back for lunch. Miranda hoped that they would come to school with her another day, but not be quite so naughty.

The Lost Ball

Once upon a time, there were three teddy bears – Mummy Teddy Bear, Daddy Teddy Bear and Baby Teddy Bear.

One day, when the sun was warm, the three teddy bears decided to go to the beach to play. They took a big ball coloured red with blue spots and plenty of hot tea and cakes.

As soon as they arrived at the beach, they kicked the ball one to another. Then Baby Teddy kicked the ball towards the sea by mistake. The ball made a big splash in the water. However, at that very moment, a large wave came along and went whoosh, whisking the ball right out to sea. Very soon there was no sign of the ball.

"Oh no" exclaimed Baby Teddy. "The ball has gone."

Large tears began to fall from Baby Teddy's eyes forming a large puddle on the pebbles on the beach. The puddle got bigger and bigger as poor baby teddy shed more tears and eventually formed a stream into the sea.

Just as Mummy and Daddy Teddy Bear were beginning to despair, there was a screeching noise from the sky above.

"It's Percy seagull" said Mummy Teddy. "Hello Percy" said Baby Teddy, "Perhaps you can help."

"Whatever is the matter?" asked Percy. Baby Teddy was still crying, but with tears still clogging up his throat, he explained about the ball. "It's right out at sea" said Daddy Teddy.

"Don't worry" said Percy, "I'll fly out to sea and look for it for you."

There was a loud flapping noise as Percy lifted his huge wings and flew up into the sky out to sea. He flew and flew over the blue waves. Occasionally a fish would jump out of the water, go "blurp" and then splash back into the water. Eventually Percy saw the ball bobbing up and down on top of the waves. He swooped down and picked up the ball into his beak and then flew back towards the beach.

The three teddy bears were so pleased to see Percy return with the ball. "Oh thank you" said Mummy Teddy.

To celebrate, the teddy bears and even Percy drank hot tea and ate up all the cakes. Then, the bears danced and sang running along the pebbles with Percy flying level with Baby Teddy's ears.

Then with a loud screech, Percy flew up into the sky and disappeared.

The three teddy bears were so tired that it was all they could do to stagger back home.

When they arrived at their little wooden house in the woods, they flopped straight into their beds and within seconds they were all fast asleep.

Baby Hazel and the Cabbage Leaf

Once upon a time, there were three squirrels – Mummy Squirrel, Daddy Squirrel and baby Hazel Squirrel.

Mummy Squirrel was very worried about Hazel who had been refusing to eat her nuts. As a result, Hazel was hungry after supper and would not sleep at night. She curled and uncurled her tail angrily at bedtime and cried all night.

One night, Mummy Squirrel could not bear it any longer. She climbed down the tree trunk where they all lived and sat under the tree sobbing.

She sobbed so much that the tears formed a small pond on the grass. Very soon a passing duck landed on the pond and swam around it. As time passed and Mummy Squirrel continued to shed large tears down her red face, the small pond got bigger and more ducks felt like making it their home. Fishes suddenly appeared in the pond, providing tasty suppers for the ducks who quacked contentedly through the night.

Well just at that moment, who should come along but Mrs Bunny Rabbit. "What's the matter?" said Mrs Bunny to Mummy Squirrel. "Baby Hazel will not eat her nuts"

explained a still very tearful Mummy Squirrel "and as a result is cross and will not sleep." Mrs Bunny sat down by the pond to think about it. Then suddenly she had a wonderful idea. "I expect Hazel is bored with the appearance of nuts" said Mrs Bunny. "Why don't you wrap some nuts in a cabbage leaf? I'll go and find you one straight away."

Mrs Bunny hopped off and returned a few minutes later with a large cabbage leaf. The caterpillars had only chomped the edges of the leaf so that there was no danger of the nuts falling out of the holes in the leaf. Mummy Squirrel put some nuts in the leaf and carefully wrapped up the nuts. She then went back up the tree to find Hazel still crying. She gave Hazel the parcel of nuts.

Well, when Hazel saw the cabbage leaf, she tossed away the nuts and chomped up every bit of the leaf.

"More, more please" she screeched. Mummy Squirrel could not believe it. She rushed down to thank Mrs Bunny.

After that Hazel had cabbage for supper every night and had no more sleepless nights.

Mummy Squirrel stopped crying, the pond got smaller and smaller, and the ducks and fishes found a new home.

To this day, Hazel, who is now quite a chubby squirrel, still prefers cabbage to nuts, but nobody minds at all.

Baby Teddy's Sunflower

O nce upon a time there was a teddy called Baby Teddy.
He was a very keen gardener and loved to grow flowers – with his Mummy's help of course.

One day, he decided he would like to grow a sunflower. His Mummy found a large flower pot and filled it with earth. Baby Teddy poked a seed into the earth and covered the seed with earth. He then watered the seed with the watering can.

Every day, Baby Teddy carefully watered his sunflower. One day, a shoot appeared and the stem of the plant began to grow.

The plant grew taller and taller every day but no flower appeared.

Then a very strange thing happened. The plant suddenly grew so tall that the stalk disappeared high into the sky so that you could not see the flower.

One day Baby Teddy was playing with his ball in the garden. It was a particularly windy day and the ball was small and light. Baby Teddy threw the ball high into the air and a bird who just happened to be flying overhead at the time, caught the ball in its beak and flew off.

Baby Teddy was not at all happy. He sat down on the grass and cried. Why was he always losing that ball?

Mummy Teddy saw him crying and came along to comfort him. "Don't worry." said Mummy Teddy "We'll get the ball back."

Suddenly a lot of noises could be heard coming from the direction of the sunflower plant. Birds were flying around the top of it singing noisily. One bird flew down to the ground and beckoned Baby Teddy to come up into the sky with him. "I can't fly" said Baby Teddy. Then suddenly, Mummy Teddy realised what was going on. "Baby Teddy" she said "You are small enough to climb up your sunflower plant."

Baby Teddy crawled to the plant and started to climb up it. He climbed and climbed. It was hard work. Soon, the ground below had disappeared and he could see the clouds like large lumps of cotton wool above. He could hear birds singing and chattering noisily to each other. Then he saw it, a huge beautiful yellow flower suspended amidst the clouds. There were massive yellow petals and in the centre of the flower was a huge brown lawn. Baby Teddy climbed onto the centre of the flower. Some birds were sitting there as well. But what were they doing? They were playing with his ball!

"That's my ball" exclaimed Baby Teddy. The birds seemed to laugh and then flew off tossing the ball into Baby Teddy's lap. A robin landed next to Baby Teddy and gave him a buttercup full of honeydew to drink. It was delicious, especially after all that climbing.

Baby Teddy thought it must be time to return to earth, so he held his ball under his arm and started to climb down the flower. Eventually, he could see Mummy Teddy smiling at him from below. He got down and jumped for joy. He had his ball back and Mummy Teddy was there with a large bowl of honey.

After all the excitement, Baby Teddy was very tired and was pleased to climb into his cot and go straight to sleep.

The next day Baby and Mummy Teddy went to look at the sunflower again, but it had completely gone. There was no sign of it at all in the flower pot. Baby Teddy felt sad. "Never mind" said Mummy Teddy. "We will grow another one next year." "Bye bye sunflower" said Baby Teddy "wherever you are and see you again next year."

A Visit to the Supermarket

Mummy Bunny Rabbit was not at all happy. It was autumn. Not only were the leaves falling off the trees making the ground slippery, but the usual pests were ruining the vegetables in the garden. The caterpillars had finally eaten up most of the cabbages and the maggots had chomped up the carrots. Even the lettuces had gone brown and horrible.

Mummy Bunny Rabbit had nothing at all to eat. She began to cry. However, just at that moment who should come along but Penny the rag doll. "What ever is wrong Mummy Bunny?" asked Penny. Mummy Bunny Rabbit explained that there was nothing left in the garden to eat. "Don't worry" said Penny. "We will go to the supermarket and buy some food."

Penny had a little red car. Mummy Bunny hopped into the back of the car and Penny drove off. Vroom, vroom went the car. As the car swerved and swayed from side to side, Mummy Bunny felt a little sick, but did not say anything.

Suddenly, the car made a loud screeching noise and came to a stop.

Mummy Bunny was pleased to get out of the car and hopped into a trolley which Penny pushed into the shop.

Well you can imagine everybody's surprise when they saw a bunny rabbit being pushed about in a trolley. All the customers in the shop stared and pointed at Mummy Bunny who let her ears flop down over her face to hide her embarrassment.

Eventually Penny and Mummy Bunny reached the vegetable section and put plenty of cabbages, carrots, spinach and lettuce into the trolley. By the time they reached the pay desk, Mummy Bunny had eaten most of the lettuce.

Penny paid for the vegetables and then wheeled the trolley out to the car park. Mummy Bunny hopped into the back of the car and Penny drove home at top speed.

Vroom, vroom, screech, swerve went the car and Mummy Bunny tried not to faint from fright. Her whiskers were shaking and she started eating the carrots to avoid looking at the frightened pedestrians Penny nearly ran over.

At last they arrived home and Mummy Bunny thanked Penny for the ride.

Mummy Bunny had enough vegetables to keep her happy for a long time. She decided she would hop her way to the supermarket next time.

A Visit to Grandma

One day, Mummy Squirrel, Daddy Squirrel and Hazel Squirrel decided to go and visit Grandma Squirrel.

Baby Hazel had wrapped up some young nuts in a large leaf as a present for Grandma Squirrel.

The three squirrels came down from their home on top of a nut tree and ran across several gardens until they came to the garden where Grandma Squirrel lived.

They came to a very old oak tree which was much older than even Grandma Squirrel. Daddy squirrel knocked at the bottom of the tree trunk with his fist – "a ratta tat tat."

The three squirrels then climbed up the tree until they came to Grandma Squirrel's front door. "Knock knock" went Hazel Squirrel.

As a croaky voice whispered "Come in", the door creaked slowly open as if it were a hundred years old.

Grandma Squirrel's house was just one room crammed with wooden furniture which was clearly much too big for the room. Grandma Squirrel sat hunched over in a large wooden rocking chair. She was wearing black rimmed glasses and was reading a book about the different varieties of nuts.

"Hello, hello, hello" said the three squirrels.

"Hello" replied Grandma Squirrel. "Do sit down and have some nut tea and nut cakes."

Hazel Squirrel liked visiting Grandma Squirrel. Her cakes were always delicious and she always told wonderful stories.

Hazel gave the present to grandma. "Oh lovely" said grandma. "These young nuts are so easy to eat. My teeth are not so good these days you know."

Over tea, grandma began one of her wonderful stories. It was the one about the woodpecker.

After tea, grandma suddenly became very tired. This was because she could not take too much excitement at her age. The three squirrels sensing her fatigue said it must be time to go and all gave grandma a big kiss as they said goodbye.

By the time the three squirrels had run all the way home, they were quite tired and were pleased to climb into their beds. Perhaps it was the nut tea! Within a few seconds, they were all fast asleep.

The Hole in the Pine Tree

Hazel Squirrel and Cornelius Bunny Rabbit played together everyday in the garden. There was one particular tree which they would often sit under when it rained. It was a large pine tree and Hazel would run after the occasional pine nut which fell from the tree.

One day Hazel rushed up to Cornelius in a very excited voice "Something has happened to the large pine tree. A small hole has appeared in the tree and there has been a lot of activity around the tree."

Cornelius and Hazel went up to the tree to examine it. Sure enough at the bottom of the trunk of the tree was a small hole and around the tree leaves had been disturbed.

"I think somebody has moved in" said Cornelius. "Whoever can it be?" said Hazel. "It is too small a hole for a bunny rabbit and even a squirrel like me would get stuck half way through that hole."

After that, Hazel and Cornelius kept a careful watch on the tree but whoever was living there was being careful not to be observed.

One day, Cornelius decided that he could not stand the suspense any longer. He went up to the pine tree and gave a

loud knock on the tree trunk just above the hole. "Rata tat tat" he went. "Hello, is anyone home?" he shouted. After a few minutes a small nose appeared through the hole. It was a nose like any other nose though quite small. "Hello nose" said Hazel. "My name is Hazel Squirrel and this is Cornelius Bunny Rabbit." Then the nose disappeared and two pink eyes appeared. The eyes were also small like the nose. Then the eyes disappeared and there was a distinct squeaking noise followed by a little mousey face popping out through the hole. "Hello" said the mouse. "Pleased to meet you. Would you like to come in and have some tea?" Cornelius and Hazel looked at each other in horror. They knew they could not possibly fit through that hole in the tree. "We are too big to fit through your front door" exclaimed Cornelius. "Try the back door" replied the mouse.

There was a scuffling noise as the mouse disappeared from sight and movements could be heard coming from the back of the tree. Then there was a squeak and a mousey voice said "Come in through the back door." Cornelius and Hazel went behind the tree to see that a hole had been uncovered in the leaves behind the tree.

It was a hole big enough even for a plump bunny rabbit.

Cornelius and Hazel approached the mouse's back door. They stepped down into the clearing in the leaves to discover a long corridor inside the tree. The mouse, who was ahead of them beckoned them to follow him. Soon they came to a door which the mouse opened and they all went into a small room. In the room were a few old chairs and a kettle. "Please sit down" said the mouse. They all sat down and were soon chatting happily over a lovely cup of tea.

Time always goes extremely fast when you are enjoying yourself and it was soon time to say goodbye.

A few days later Cornelius knocked on the tree by the back door, but everything was quiet. He noticed that the leaves had gone and there was no hole anymore. Cornelius was just beginning to feel sad when a little voice behind him made him jump. "Hello." It was the mouse. "I have moved house" explained the mouse. "I have moved in with Mrs Mouse in the next garden where there is much more room for two mice. Why don't you visit us next week?"

Cornelius decided that he would very definitely visit the mice next week and he might even take Hazel Squirrel.